Salma
the
Syrian Chef

Story by **Danny Ramadan**

Art by **Anna Bron**

annick press
toronto • berkeley

Salma watches the Vancouver rain from her apartment window in the Welcome Center. It's different than the sunny days back in Syria.

She still can't pronounce "Vancouver," but her friends tell her that her ways of saying it are more fun.

"Fankoufer," Salma says to Mama, but Mama is making dinner.

"Vandourar." Salma rolls her Rs, but Mama won't look up from her English homework.

"Vancouver!" Salma finally succeeds, but Mama is busy calling Papa back in Syria.

Papa will join them in Canada soon.

Salma's heart aches like a tiny fire in her chest when she thinks of Papa. She wonders if Mama's heart is burning too.

Mama used to giggle with her friends in the refugee camp.
It sounded like the ringing bells on the older boys' bikes.

Now, after a long day of job interviews and English classes,
Mama barely smiles when tucking Salma in.

Maybe if Salma can make Mama laugh,
Vancouver will feel a little more like home.

Salma draws Mama a clown balancing
on a ball on top of an elephant.

She tells Mama a knock-knock joke
about bananas and oranges that
she learned in language school.

She even hides behind the fridge.
She jumps out and screams, "Boo!"

But all she gets is Mama's sad smile,
full of love but empty of joy.

"I want to make Mama laugh!" Salma rushes into the playroom and almost crashes into Nancy's chair. "She's been sad for a long time."

"When was the last time you saw Mama happy?" asks Nancy in her broken Arabic.

Salma imagines a waterfall of Mama's many sad faces since they left Syria.

"How about you draw a picture?" Nancy says.
"Drawing helps me when I forget my good memories."

Salma looks at the colorful crayons. Her memories of Mama's
smile shine like a beautiful rainbow over that waterfall.

Salma draws her home back in Damascus: a yellow house with a garden surrounding it like a necklace.

The garden had a tree with green leaves and a bird's nest with three little eggs.

She colors the living room walls purple.

"Were the walls really purple?" Nancy asks.

"No," Salma says, "But it's okay to add new colors to my own memories."

She draws Papa at the table. Mama carries a freshly-made dish of foul shami, a big smile on her face.

Salma can't bring Papa here sooner.

She can't rebuild their old home.

But suddenly, she knows what to do.

"I think Mama misses Syrian food," Salma tells Nancy and the other kids. "I want to make her foul shami."

"I miss kushari," Ayman says. Salma tastes the salty, spicy Egyptian dish on her tongue.

"I miss the way my mama made masala dosa back in India," Riya adds.

Evan misses arepas. He just arrived from Venezuela.

But none of them have heard of foul shami, and Salma doesn't know how to make it.

"Do you know how to make foul shami?" Salma asks Jad, the Jordanian translator who taught her the English names of the flowers in the community garden.

"No, but I can find a recipe for you," Jad says. His fingers move swiftly on his keyboard, then Salma hears the printer ticking.

Jad hands Salma a paper with Arabic words.

"I can do this," she whispers.

Then she realizes: she doesn't know the
English names of any vegetables!

Salma reads the Arabic words. She is scared of looking silly
in this new place where hardly anyone knows her language.

The smell of crayon on her hands reminds her:
"I can draw the vegetables!"

"Yellow for lemon, green for parsley, brown for peas and red for onions," she sings. "And this is chickpeas and that's garlic, and that's a bottle of olive oil."

Soon, she has all the drawings she needs.

Ayesha walks Salma to the supermarket,
so she doesn't have to cross the street alone.

Salma likes Ayesha: they play hopscotch in the Welcome Center,
and Ayesha brought her home-baked Somalian sweets.

"*Shukran.*" Salma thanks Ayesha as they wait for the traffic to stop.

Back at the Welcome Center, Salma organizes her vegetables on the kitchen table.

"My mama won't be laughing at all if I use a knife," Salma tells Amir and Malek, who came together from Lebanon. "Can you help me chop these vegetables?"

She blushes when Malek kisses away Amir's onion tears.
The three of them giggle . . . until Salma realizes she forgot the spices.

"Mama likes sumac with her foul shami!"

Salma looks through the spice rack.

Paprika is Papa's favorite spice, and Mama loves cardamom in her coffee.

Pepper makes her sneeze.

But she can't find sumac!

Tears fill her eyes. "This is the worst idea ever! It's too hard to cook Syrian food here."

Salma's fingers shake. The spices get blurry and their smells mix together.

"Everything is ruined," Salma says between her teeth. "I'll never make Mama laugh!"

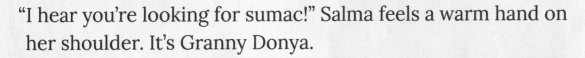

"I hear you're looking for sumac!" Salma feels a warm hand on her shoulder. It's Granny Donya.

"I miss Persian cooking, too," Granny says, handing Salma a tiny red jar. "Family dinners back in Iran always made me happy."

"I'm mad that we had to leave home," Salma insists.
"I can't find sumac or speak Arabic to everyone I know."

"Look at those beautiful flowers and all those blossoming trees."
Granny Donya points out the window. "This home might be
different from everything we know, but it's beautiful in its own ways."

Salma takes a deep breath, filled with the smell of sumac and rain.
Her anger escapes a little, like water droplets flying off her hands
when she shakes them dry.

Salma sprinkles Granny Donya's sumac into the foul shami.

"It is beautiful," she agrees.

"One final step!" Salma holds the olive oil bottle over the bowl, but it slips out of her hand and crashes to the floor.

Amir and Malek help her clean up the glass, but they have no olive oil for her to use.

Ayesha has never cooked with olive oil before.

Granny Donya's bottle is empty.

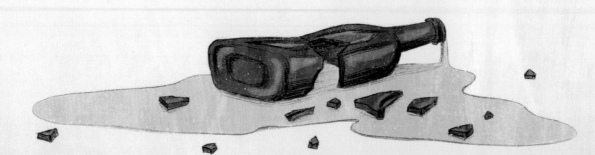

Salma used her money on the other
groceries, so she can't buy more!

She sits on the floor and cries.

Salma feels useless, like an umbrella in a country with no rain.

She hides her teary face when Nancy walks by.
Nancy stops beside her. "What's wrong?"

"Everything," Salma says. "All I wanted was to
make Mama laugh, and look at the mess I made."

"What I see is a dish made with love," Nancy whispers. "I don't think it's missing a thing."

When Mama comes home that night, Salma blocks her way into the apartment. "Don't be mad!"

Mama frowns. "What happened?"

Salma opens the door. "I couldn't find olive oil."

On the table, a bowl of foul shami awaits.

"You made this for me?" Mama asks.

Before Salma can answer, the door opens again.
"We brought olive oil," Nancy says. Salma jumps in excitement.

And then Mama breaks into a long, sweet laugh, like the echo of bells.

"Mama," Salma says while Mama tucks her in that night, "when I'm with you, I feel at home."

Mama kisses Salma goodnight. "Your smile is my home."

In her dream, Salma rides a bike around Vancouver's seawall. She rings the bell and Mama laughs beside her.

Around her, all her new friends ride their bikes and ring their bells.

Salma feels the sun on her face and looks up to a purple sky, painted with colors of crayon.

That dream goes on all night long.

To the yet-to-be-born child that one day will be mine, I love you already. —D.R.

For my mom. —A.B.

Foul shami, the Syrian dish Salma prepares for Mama, can be translated as Damascene fava beans in English. In Arabic, *foul* (pronounced "fool") means fava beans, and *shami* (pronounced "shammy") means Damascene—from the Syrian city of Damascus.

To find out how you can make foul shami, check out the recipe at
www.annickpress.com/Salma-the-Syrian-Chef

© 2020 Danny Ramadan (text)
© 2020 Anna Bron (illustrations)
Cover art/design by Anna Bron and Paul Covello
Designed by Paul Covello

Annick Press Ltd.

We acknowledge the support of the Canada Council for the Arts and the Ontario Arts Council, and the participation of the Government of Canada/la participation du gouvernement du Canada for our publishing activities.

Canada [🍁] ⊗A ONTARIO ARTS COUNCIL
CONSEIL DES ARTS DE L'ONTARIO
an Ontario government agency
un organisme du gouvernement de l'Ontario

Library and Archives Canada Cataloguing in Publication

Title: Salma the Syrian chef / story by Danny Ramadan ; art by Anna Bron
Names: Ramadan, Ahmad Danny, author. | Bron, Anna, 1989- illustrator.
Identifiers: Canadiana (print) 20190170301 | Canadiana (ebook) 20190170328 | ISBN 9781773213750 (hardcover) | ISBN 9781773213781 (PDF) | ISBN 9781773213774 (Kindle) | ISBN 9781773213767 (HTML)
Classification: LCC PS8635.A4613 S25 2020 | DDC jC813/.6—dc23

Published in the U.S.A. by Annick Press (U.S.) Ltd.
Distributed in Canada by University of Toronto Press.
Distributed in the U.S.A. by Publishers Group West.

Printed in China

annickpress.com
dannyramadan.com
annabron.com

Also available as an e-book. Please visit annickpress.com/ebooks for more details.